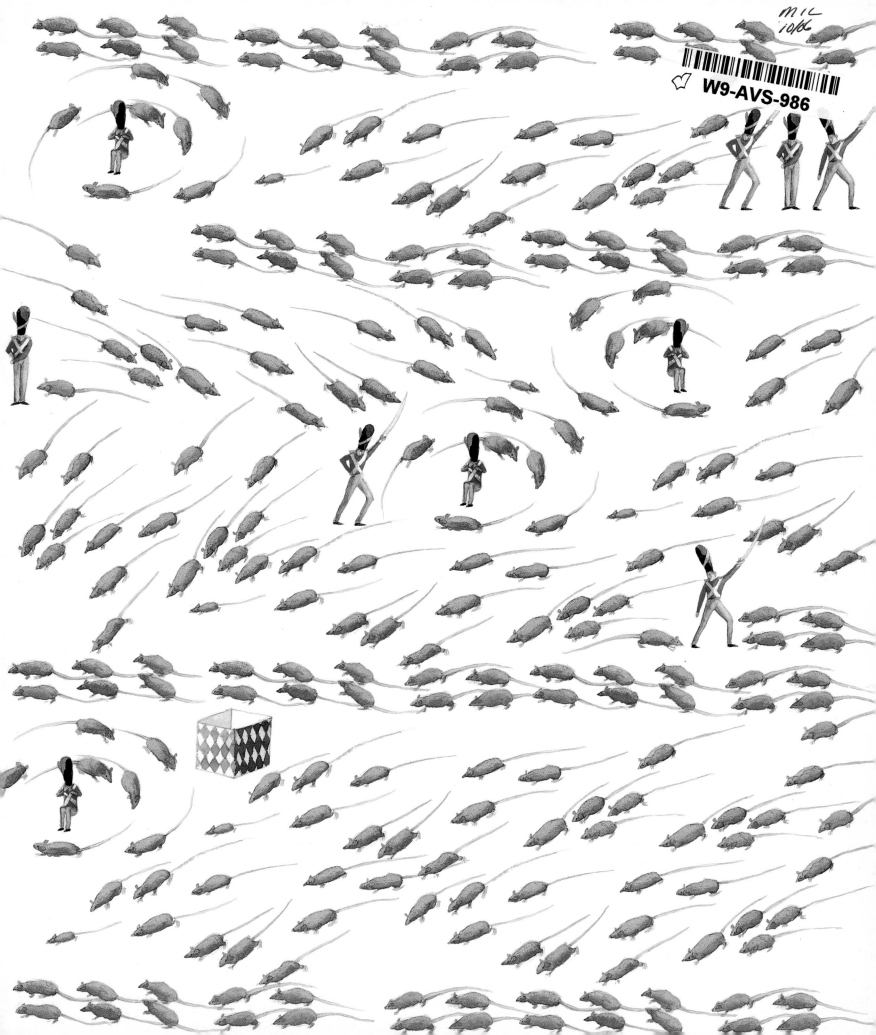

To my dentist —L.Z.

Foreword

The Nutcracker and the Mouse King—*even the name of what is surely E.T.A. Hoffmann's best-known fairy tale suggests music, images, resonant echoes. Published in 1816, this story, which skillfully weaves reality and fantasy, was written by Hoffmann for Marie Hitzig, the small daughter of one of his friends. Inspired by her imagination, he conjured up the festive mood of Christmas Eve, turning the child's home into a magical reality full of excitement and poetry. The world of the Land of Toys has its own language, and the sound of the words and the striking images bring its atmosphere to vivid life.*

E.T.A. Hoffmann's poetic power and his gift for narrative, with its irresistible wit and comedy, have made him one of the writers Lisbeth Zwerger most admires. To her, he is the Romantic poet par excellence, conjuring up pictures, stimulating the imagination. She published a version of this story in 1979, quite early in her career as an illustrator. Now, over 24 years later, she has tackled it again. Here we have an artist competing with herself—a bold and unusual venture, but one which has astonishing results.

The present version of the text was devised especially for this edition. To the great regret of all concerned, the original is too long for the picture-book format. However, this retelling aims to preserve its wit, fantasy, and verbal dexterity as much as possible. But readers who are captivated by the fantastic world of E.T.A. Hoffmann as it is depicted in this book are encouraged to read the original text. It is well worthwhile.

Susanne Koppe

E.T.A. Hoffmann

Nutcracker

Illustrated by

Lisbeth Zwerger

Retold by

Susanne Koppe

Translated from the German
by Anthea Bell

A Michael Neugebauer Book
North-South Books / New York / London

Christmas Eve was here at last.

Little Marie Stahlbaum and her brother, Fritz, had been waiting for hours in the dimly lit room next to the sitting room. What presents would they find waiting for them under the tree this year? Marie's doll, Trudy, badly needed a new dress, and . . .

At last the time had come! Lovely, soft music reached the children's ears, and they felt as if wings were fluttering in the air around them. There was no doubt about it—the Christ Child had just flown past. Then—ting-a-ling, ting-a-ling!—the big double doors opened.

The bright light from the sitting room shone in the children's eyes. Dazed, they hesitated in the doorway for a moment—and then ran to the Christmas tree.

"Oh, oh, oh!" Marie kept crying, and Fritz jumped for joy. What fine presents they had! Marie found a doll's tea set and a new doll and immediately decided to call her Clara. Fritz was delighted with his brightly painted toy soldiers.

Both children had presents of picture books and sugar candy, and there was a wonderful mechanical toy made by their godfather, Councillor Drosselmeier himself. He gave them one every year. This time it was a magnificent castle with a tiny chandelier hanging in it, burning real candles, and a little doll was waving from one window.

But you couldn't really play with the castle, so Fritz soon lined up his soldiers on parade, while Marie went on looking at all her own presents. Suddenly, she saw the figure of a little man under the tree. He wasn't very showy, so she had missed seeing him before. His head was almost as big as his spindly body, which made him look rather odd, but to make up for that he wore a pretty little coat and had a beautiful white beard. There was a kind, friendly expression in his pale green eyes.

"Oh," said Marie, "whose is that dear little man?"

"He's going to crack hard nuts for us," said her father. "He belongs to us all—but if you like him so much I'll let you look after him. Take good care of the nutcracker."

"Awake, awake—we go to fight—this very night we go to fight—awake, awake, a warlike sight!" came the war cry from the cupboard, and one by one the toy soldiers climbed out of their boxes, while Nutcracker took a bold leap and jumped into the drawer at the bottom of the cupboard.

"Strike up a march to summon the troops, my faithful drummer boy!" he shouted, and the army marched out with banners flying and a loud fanfare. At the same time, a squeaking and a squealing could be heard in the room—the eyes of hordes of mice were flashing, and the dreadful seven-headed mouse towered above them all.

Bang! Bang! Bang! went the guns of Nutcracker's army as they fired sugar plums and ginger nuts at the mice. But more and more mice came, taking good aim and slinging white pills at the toy soldiers.

All was in confusion. The Mouse King and his mice kept squeaking, and now and then Nutcracker's powerful voice rang out. Some of the cavalry bravely threw themselves into battle, but Fritz's hussars were not quite so bold. The ugly, evil-smelling bullets fired at them by the mice soiled their smart tunics, and they swerved aside and ran away. It wasn't long before a great troop of mice was putting the other soldiers to flight, too. Nutcracker, with a last little loyal band of toys, was fighting desperately in front of the glass-fronted cupboard. Then up came the Mouse King, with his seven mouths uttering seven cries of triumph.

"Oh, my poor Nutcracker!" sobbed Marie, and without stopping to think she threw her left shoe into the army of mice, aiming straight for their king. At that moment all fell still, and everyone seemed to have scattered and fled.

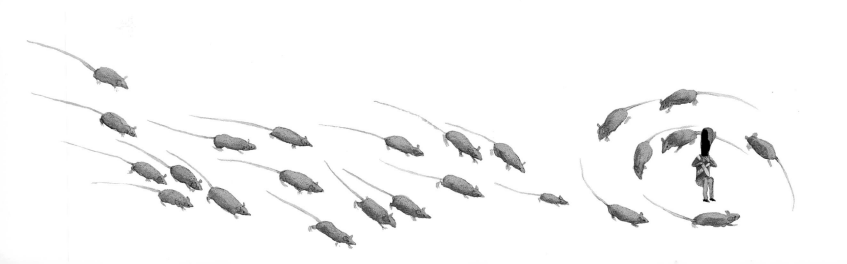

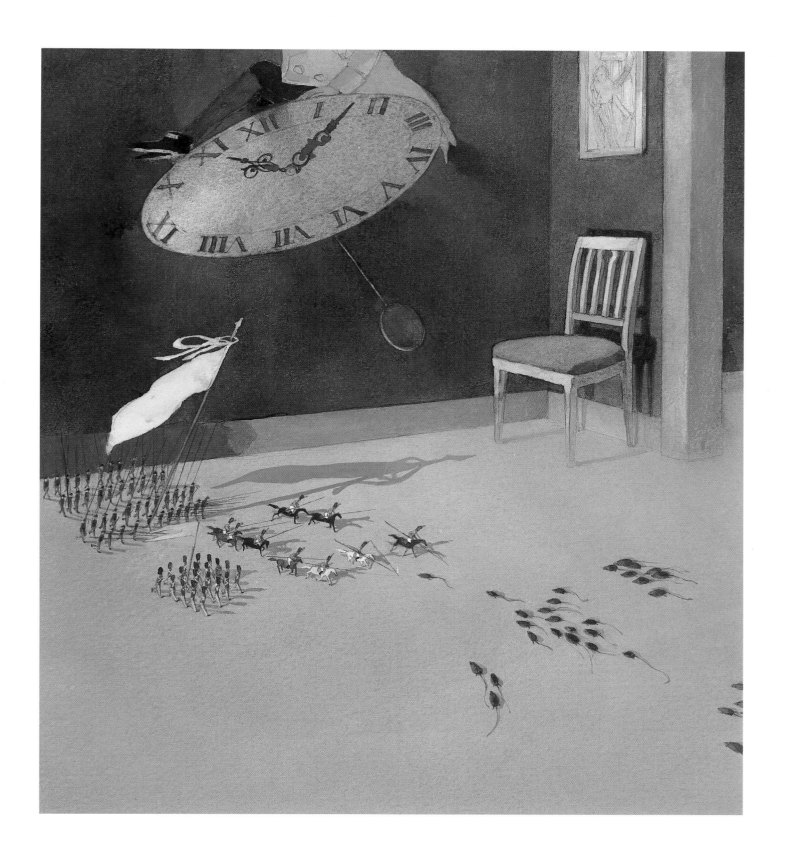

The sun shone brightly through the window, which was frosted up outside. When Marie opened her eyes she was looking at her mother's anxious face. "Oh, have those ugly mice gone away?" asked Marie. "And is Nutcracker safe?"

"My goodness, Marie," said her mother, "what does our nutcracker have to do with mice? But perhaps it was a mouse that frightened you yesterday and made you put your arm through the glass of the cupboard door. Thank goodness I woke at midnight and discovered that you weren't in bed. And where did I find you? Lying there bleeding and holding the nutcracker—with the toy soldiers scattered around you, and your left shoe in the middle of them all."

"Oh, Mother," cried Marie, "that was the great battlefield where the toys and the mice had been fighting!"

"Now, Marie, do calm down," said her mother gently. "All the mice have gone away, and the nutcracker's safe in the cupboard."

Marie was running a high temperature, and she had to stay in bed for several days. But she knew that Nutcracker had been rescued, and sometimes, as if in a dream, she thought she heard him say: "Marie, dear lady, I owe you so much. But you can do even more for me!"

What might that be? Marie couldn't solve the puzzle.

Then, one afternoon when she was bored with being sick in bed, the door opened and in came Godfather Drosselmeier.

"I wanted to see how the poor invalid is doing," he said.

"Godfather Drosselmeier," Marie burst out, "why didn't you come down from the clock and help Nutcracker?"

"Marie!" cried her horrified mother.

But her godfather only made a very odd face and hummed, "Clocks, clock, tick, tick, tock—to join the fight would not be right."

"Mr. Drosselmeier!" said her mother sternly.

Marie's godfather quickly sat down on the edge of her bed and whispered. "Oh, I'd happily have pecked out all the Mouse King's 14 eyes, but that would never do! Here's something nice, though: see what I've brought you!"

And so saying, he produced Nutcracker. He had repaired his jaw and given him nice new teeth. Marie shouted for joy, and her godfather smiled. "He's no beauty," he told the child. "But if you like I'll tell you why he looks that way. Or do you know the tale of Princess Pirlipat already?"

"No," said Marie, and she and Fritz, who had come into the room, too, both cried, "Tell us, Godfather Drosselmeier, tell us the story!"

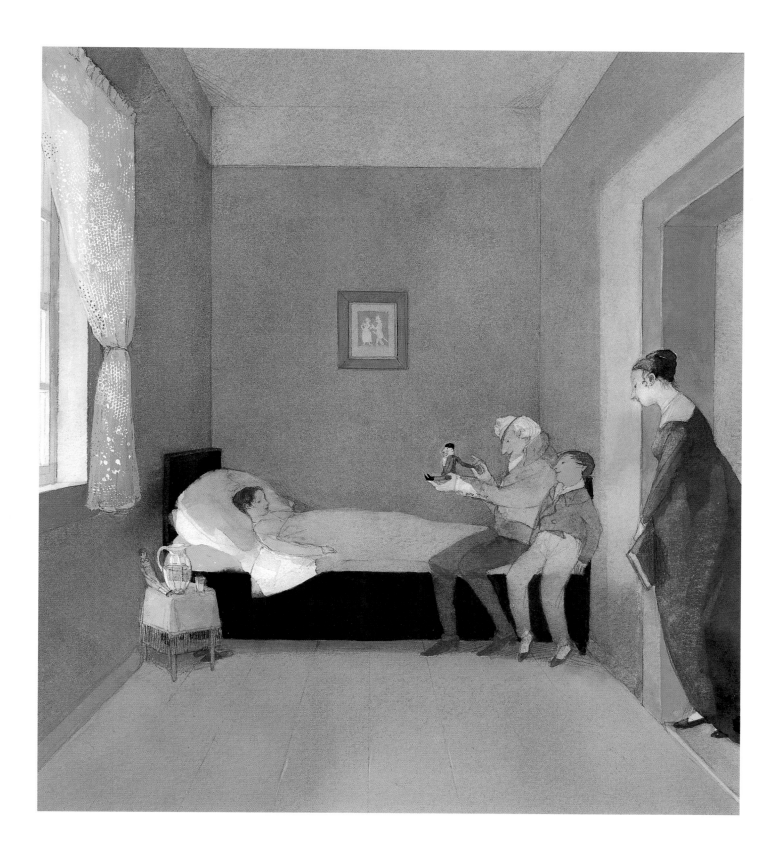

When Princess Pirlipat came into the world her father, the king, was beside himself with joy.

"Hurray," he kept crying, "did anyone ever see anything lovelier than my little Pirlipatty?" And all the ministers, generals, and high-ranking officers agreed with him. It was a fact that there had never been a prettier child than Princess Pirlipat: her little face might have been woven of silk as white as a lily and as red as a rose, her eyes were sparkling azure blue, and her hair was like curly gold thread. Furthermore, Pirlipat had come into the world complete with two rows of pearly little teeth, and two hours after she was born she bit the Lord Chancellor with them.

Everyone was happy except for the queen, who seemed anxious and uneasy. She had the child carefully guarded, and six ladies-in-waiting had to sit in her room at night, each with a cat on her lap. No one knew why—but I am about to tell you.

It so happened that a little while before the baby's birth, a great feast of sausages had been held at the court of Pirlipat's father. The king loved nothing more than sausages, so the queen herself presided over the golden pan in which they were cooking. When she came to the most important part of the sausage-making, frying the bacon, a tiny little whisper of a voice was heard: "Give me some bacon, sister! I want to join the feast! I'm a queen myself!"

The queen knew who the speaker was at once—Mistress Mousie, who claimed to be ruler of the land of Mousolia. The queen was happy to oblige her, but no sooner had she offered her a little bacon than up scurried Mistress Mousie's whole huge family, including her seven big, bad sons, and they all wanted to share in the banquet. The Mistress of Ceremonies shooed the gang of mice away—but too late.

"Not enough bacon!" said the king when he sat down to eat his sausages, and the feast was quite spoiled for him.

The king swore revenge, and that revenge was to be taken by his Court Clockmaker Christian Elias Drosselmeier—yes, his name was just the same as mine. Using fried bacon as bait, the Clockmaker set mousetraps to get rid of Mistress Mousie and all her people forever. In spite of all clever Mistress Mousie's warnings, mouse after mouse came to a sad end in the traps. Mistress Mousie herself was so grief-stricken that she left her kingdom. But before turning her back on the royal court she told the queen: "My sons are dead. So take care, Madam Queen, take care that Queen Mousie doesn't bite your own little princess in two!"

One night, one of Princess Pirlipat's ladies-in-waiting happened to wake from a deep sleep at midnight. She saw an ugly great mouse sitting beside the baby's head and jumped up with a shriek, which alarmed the cats in the room. They tried to catch Mistress Mousie—for it was she—but in vain—she had disappeared.

All the noise made Pirlipat wake up, crying.

"Thank heaven!" cried the ladies-in-waiting. "She's alive!"

But what had happened to Pirlipat? Her pretty, angelic face was all shapeless now, her graceful body was crooked, her blue eyes were green and staring, and her little mouth stretched from ear to ear.

The queen was ready to die of grief, and the king's room had to be lined with padded wallpaper, because he kept knocking his head against the wall and wailing, "Oh, what an unhappy monarch I am!"

In his misery the king summoned the Court Clockmaker. "Christian Elias Drosselmeier," he said—for you'll remember that the Court Clockmaker shared my name—"cure the princess or you must die!"

Drosselmeier shed bitter tears, while the princess happily cracked nut after nut. A nut, thought the Court Clockmaker suddenly, that's the clue!

Hadn't the princess come into the world with teeth in her head already? And since her transformation, hadn't she shown a remarkable craving for nuts?

In his excitement, Drosselmeier went to see his best friend, the Court Astronomer, who cast the princess's horoscope. It was very complicated, for the lines of fate were tangled and difficult to decipher. But in the end all was clear—to be as beautiful as before, the princess must eat the sweet kernel of the Crackatuck nut, once a young man had cracked it with his own teeth and handed it to her with his eyes closed. Then he must take seven steps backward—and only then might he open his eyes again.

The king was delighted. His daughter would have her beauty back! But where in the world was the Crackatuck nut to be found? Or a young man who could crack it with his teeth? For that nut had such a hard shell that a 48-pounder cannon could roll over it without cracking its shell.

The queen thought of advertising for such a young man in the newspapers. The king's idea was to send the Court Clockmaker and the Court Astronomer to find the Crackatuck nut—wherever it might be.

Drosselmeier and the Astronomer had been journeying around the world for 15 years when they both felt very homesick all of a sudden, so they came straight back from Asia to Nuremberg, where the Court Clockmaker's cousin lived, a dollmaker called Christoph Zacharias Drosselmeier.

"Hm," said the dollmaker, "I think I can help you!" And he showed them a gilded nut that he had bought years ago at a very high price from a strange nut-seller. They made haste to rub the gilding off, and underneath they clearly saw the name of the nut written in Chinese characters saying Crackatuck.

"Good things seldom come singly," said the Astronomer. "The stars tell me that we've found not only the nut but the young man to crack it. He's your cousin's son!"

The cousin's son was a handsome youth who used to stand in his father's workshop, very kindly cracking nuts for the girls. You hardly noticed that he had once been a jumping jack.

When news that the nut had been found became known many young man, trusting in their strong jaws, tried to break the spell on the princess. But one after another, they found it was their teeth they broke instead. Then young Drosselmeier presented himself. He broke the nutshell with a single crack! and handed it to the princess with his eyes closed.

No sooner had she eaten the kernel than she turned into a lovely young woman of angelic beauty. To fulfil the prophecy, all young Drosselmeier had to do now was take seven steps backward. He had taken six, but at the seventh he stumbled over Mistress Mousie—and oh, what a misfortune, now he looked just as the princess had looked before!

"Nutcracker sly," squeaked the dying mouse, "soon you must die! My death will be avenged, don't doubt—my mouse king son will pay you out!"

When the princess saw how young Drosselmeier had been transformed, she was so horrified that the man who had saved her was banished from court, along with his two companions.

The stars had failed to tell the Astronomer about that. But he cast a new horoscope and discovered that young Drosselmeier would be prince and then king some day—that is, if he could defeat Mistress Mousie's seven-headed son and win the love of a lady in spite of his odd looks.

"There, dear children," Godfather Drosselmeier ended his story, "now you know why people so often say, 'That was a hard nut to crack!' and why nutcrackers are so ugly."

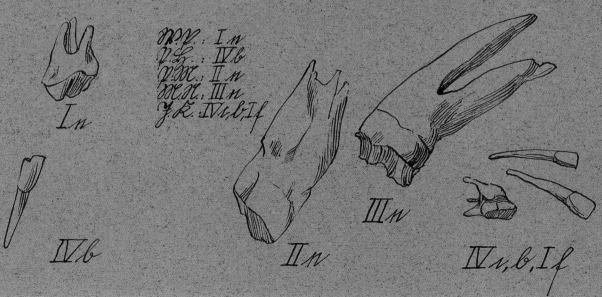

At last Marie was allowed to get up again, and she hurried to the glass-fronted cupboard. There stood her dear Nutcracker. "I'll take care of you!" she whispered to him. "But oh dear, why didn't your uncle help you?"

When Godfather Drosselmeier next came to tea, she told him to his face: "Now I know you're the banished Court Clockmaker and Nutcracker is your nephew and at war with Mistress Mousie's son. Why don't you help him?"

The whole family laughed at Marie. What strange fancies she took into her head! But her godfather whispered to her, "Ah, you alone—you alone can save him!"

Not long after that, Marie heard a loud noise in her room one night. "Oh, the mice, the mice are coming back!" she cried in alarm, unable to move. Eyes and crowns flashing, the Mouse King burrowed through a hole in the wall, and with a mighty bound he landed on Marie's little bedside table.

"You must give me your sugar plums and marzipan," he squealed, "or I'll bite your little nutcracker in two."

In the morning, Marie's mother said in surprise, "I don't know how the mice get into our living room. Poor Marie! Just look, they've eaten all your marzipan!"

Marie didn't mind. Nutcracker was safe now, she thought.

But next night there was a squeaking and a squealing in her ear again, "Give me your sugar dollies or I'll bite Nutcracker in two!"

When Marie's mother found the nibbled dollies next day she cried, "There must be a horrible mouse at large here!" And she set a mousetrap baited with fried bacon. But even that didn't help.

The next night Marie heard squealing again, "Hand them over—your books and your dress, I must have them, oh yes! If you will not let them go, I'll bite Nutcracker in two."

"Oh, dear me!" wailed Marie next morning. "What am I to do?" She went to the glass-fronted cupboard and took out Nutcracker. In her arms, he began to get warm and to move. "A sword," he whispered creakily, "a sword!"

Marie jumped for joy. At last she knew how to help him! She borrowed a sword from Fritz's soldiers. She could hardly sleep next night, she was so anxious. There was a lot of noise outside, then a squeak—and then came a knock at the door.

"Dear Miss Stahlbaum," she heard a voice outside call, "good news! The wicked Mouse King is defeated!" It sounded just like young Mr. Drosselmeier, but when the door opened, it was Nutcracker who entered and gave Marie seven little golden crowns.

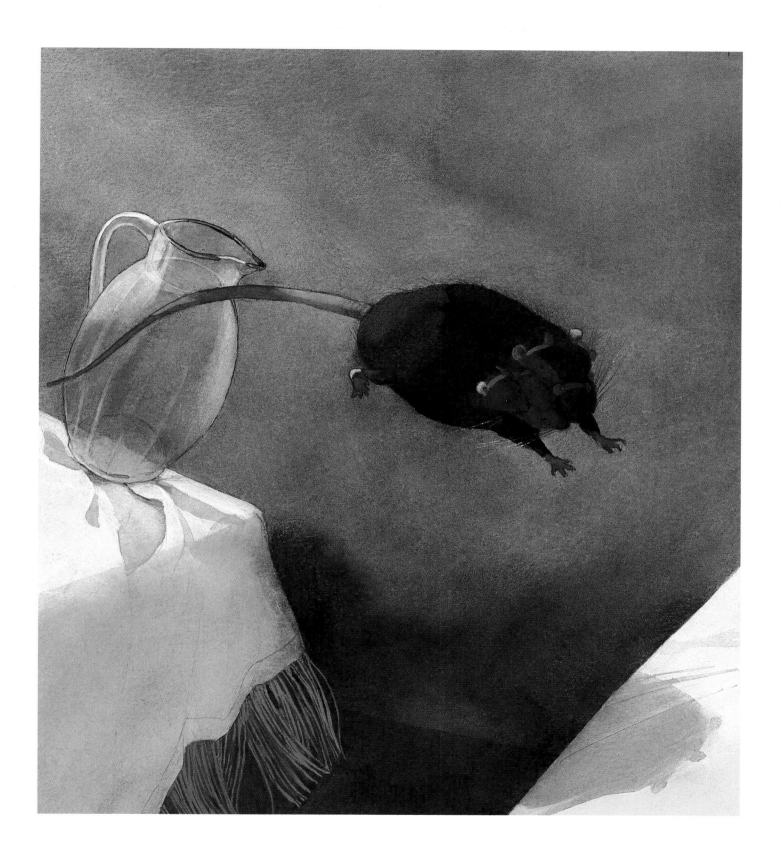

"Only your help," said Nutcracker, "gave me courage and strength for the battle. As a way of thanking you, I'd like to show you some wonderful things—will you follow me?"

"I will certainly go with you," said Marie, "but it mustn't be far and it mustn't take long, because I haven't had my night's sleep yet."

"In that case," he replied, "I'll choose the nearest way, although it's a little difficult."

He led Marie over to the massive old wardrobe in the hall of the house. The door of the wardrobe was open, and Nutcracker clambered nimbly up the ornamental carving. Once he had scaled the wardrobe he pulled a tassel, and a pretty little stairway came down through the sleeve of Father's overcoat.

"Just keep climbing up, dear young lady," said Nutcracker.

Marie did as he said. No sooner had she emerged from the top of the sleeve than bright light shone in her face, and she found that she was standing in a wonderfully fragrant meadow full of sparkling precious stones.

"This is Rock Candy Meadow," said Nutcracker.

Together they went through a gateway made of almonds and raisins, with a gallery above it where six little monkeys in red jackets were playing music. To the sound of their beautiful tunes, Nutcracker and Marie went on into a little wood with wonderful scents wafting out of it.

Golden fruit hung from bright branches in the wood, shining and sparkling among the leaves. The trees had decked themselves out with ribbons and bunches of flowers, like merry wedding guests and bridesmaids, and at every breath of wind there was a rustling in the branches and leaves, and tinsel crackled and crinkled with a cheerful musical sound.

"Oh, it's lovely!" cried Marie, delighted.

"We are in Christmas Wood," said Nutcracker.

"Can we stay here for a little while?" asked Marie.

Nutcracker clapped his hands, and immediately along came a number of shepherds and shepherdesses, hunters and huntresses. They were so white and delicate that they might have been made of pure sugar. Marie sat in an armchair to watch them performing a beautiful ballet.

After the dancing, they went on past Orange Brook, which smelled delicious, past Lemonade Cascade, and finally along the slow-flowing Honey River. Picturesque Gingerbread Village lay on its banks. They walked through a little town of bright, translucent houses made of sugar candy, and beyond it they came to Rose Lake, where silver waves splashed melodiously.

"Oh, how lovely," cried Marie. "It might have been made by Godfather Drosselmeier himself!"

"No, no, dear young lady," said Nutcracker. "My uncle can't make anything as good as this—you do it much better!"

He clapped his hands, and two boats in the shape of shells drawn by dolphins came toward them. They glided gently across the lake in the shell-shaped boats.

What a sight met Marie's eyes on the opposite bank—and how can I describe it to you? Beyond glittering bushes and magnificent beds of flowers rose the capital city, with walls and towers in wonderful hues. And as for the shapes of the houses, nothing like them was to be seen anywhere else on earth, they were so unusual.

As they passed through the city gate, the soldiers presented arms. "Welcome, dear Prince," they cried, "welcome to Candy City!"

Marie was surprised to find that Nutcracker was a prince here—and even more surprised by the happy chatter, the rejoicing, and laughter in all the streets. "Dear young lady," explained Nutcracker, "this is nothing unusual. Candy City is a merry town. It's like this every day."

Suddenly a dignified man made his way through the crowd. "Confectioner, Confectioner!" he kept shouting, and at once the noise died down a little.

"What was that about?" asked Marie.

"Confectioner is the name of an unknown but terrible power. It can make the people of Candy City into anything it likes! It and Giant Sweet Tooth are the only threat to our city."

Suddenly Marie and Nutcracker were standing in front of a castle bathed in glowing pink light, with hundreds of fantastic turrets. "This is Marzipan Castle," said Nutcracker, leading Marie through the entrance.

Inside, four princesses in beautiful dresses were waiting for Nutcracker. "How have you been?" they asked as they welcomed their brother.

Nutcracker took Marie's hand. "This," he said, "is Miss Marie Stahlbaum, who saved my life! If she hadn't thrown her shoe and then found me a sword, the terrible Mouse King would have bitten me in two."

And he told the whole story from the beginning: the toy soldiers and the battle, the Mouse King's blackmail of Marie, and her brave defiance. But the more he talked, the further away his voice seemed to be.

It seemed to Marie as if faint veils of mist were rising, and the princesses and Nutcracker were dissolving in the mist. A strange singing and whirring and humming was heard, and as if on rolling waves Marie rose higher . . . and higher . . . and higher . . .

Marie fell from a great height. Then she was lying in her bed in broad daylight, and there stood her mother saying, "How can anyone sleep so long?"

Marie must have fallen asleep in Marzipan Castle and been carried home. She told her mother all about her adventures and the sights she had seen.

"Marie," said her mother, "you've had a lovely long dream—but now put it out of your head. Look," and she went over to the glass-fronted cupboard, "there's your beloved Nutcracker, and he can't move."

No one would believe Marie's stories, but the pictures of the wonderful fairy kingdom remained vivid in her mind, and she kept looking dreamily at the glass-fronted cupboard. "Oh, dear Mr Drosselmeier," she said one day, "if only you were really alive I wouldn't scorn you as Princess Pirlipat did—never mind whether you were ugly or not!"

At that moment there was such a bang and a jolt that Marie fainted away and fell off her chair. When she came to she heard her mother calling, "Marie, we have visitors!"

There stood her godfather and, behind him, a handsome young man in a red-and-gold coat—his nephew from Nuremberg. He showed how well brought up he was by bringing pretty presents—a sword for Fritz and for Marie sugar dolls just like those that the Mouse King had nibbled. And at dinner he cracked nuts for everyone. Crack!—and the nutshells were open.

After dinner he asked Marie to show him the glass-fronted cupboard. "Most excellent Miss Stahlbaum," he said, falling on his knees before her, "the moment you said you wouldn't scorn me like mean-minded Princess Pirlipat I returned to my old shape. Dear young lady, give me your hand and make me happy, share my crown and kingdom, and come to Marzipan Castle with me."

"Dear Mr. Drosselmeier," replied Marie, "you are a kind man and you rule a lovely country. I will happily marry you!"

So now Marie was engaged to marry young Mr. Drosselmeier, and a year later he came to fetch her in his golden coach drawn by silver horses. They say that to this day she is queen of the land where you may see glittering Christmas Woods, translucent Marzipan Castles, and the most wonderful and beautiful things—if only you have eyes for them. And that's the end of the tale of Nutcracker and the Mouse King.

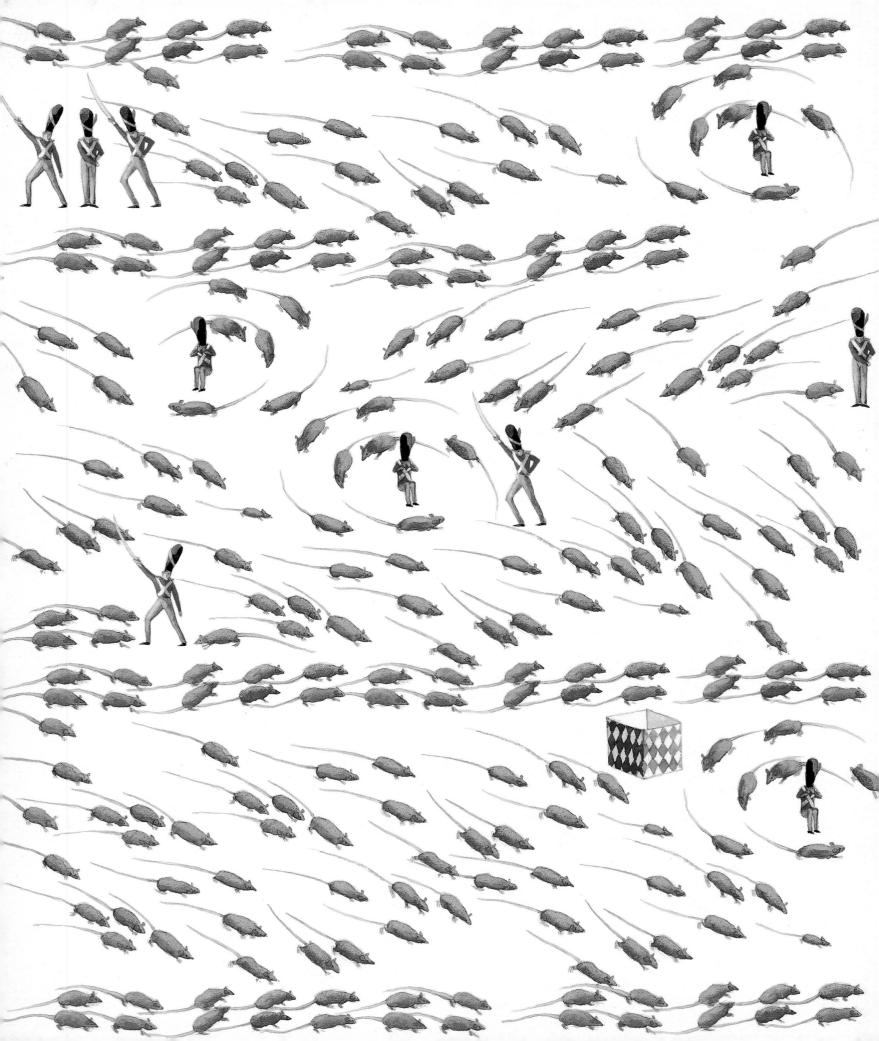